" 'Grand opening'," Alfred read from the newspaper. " 'Grand opening today of Pedro's Pasta Pizza Place. Bring the family! There's fun for all — and the world's largest——"

"Go on!" said Alistair excitedly.

"The world's largest...PIZZA!" Alfred exclaimed.

"The only problem," said Alistair, "is pinching the blooming thing. But as usual, Alfred, your brainy brother has come up with a brilliant plan. Now, come over here and I'll whisper what it is..."

Also available in Young Lions

Simon and the Witch *Margaret Stuart Barry*
Paddington at Large *Michael Bond*
Fancy Nancy in Disguise *Ruth Craft*
The Reluctant Dragon *Kenneth Grahame*
Holiday with the Fiend *Sheila Lavelle*
Wheel of Danger *Robert Leeson*
Josie Smith *Magdalen Nabb*
Josie Smith at School *Magdalen Nabb*
Josie Smith at the Seaside *Magdalen Nabb*
Journey to Jo'Burg *Beverley Naidoo*
Salford Road and Other Poems *Gareth Owen*
Mind Your Own Business *Michael Rosen*
Out of the Blue *Fiona Waters*

J. J. Murhall

Eddie and the Swine Family

Illustrated by Tony Blundell

Young Lions
An Imprint of HarperCollins *Publishers*

For Michael and
Saoirse Ruby -

With love and many thanks

First published in Great Britain in Young Lions 1994
1 3 5 7 9 10 8 6 4 2

Young Lions is an imprint of the Children's Division,
part of HarperCollins Publishers Ltd,
77/85 Fulham Palace Road, Hammersmith,
London W6 8JB

Copyright © Jacqui J. Murhall 1994
Illustrations copyright © Tony Blundell 1994

The author asserts the moral right to be
identified as the author of this work.

ISBN 0 00 674726-4

Set in Educational Century
Printed and bound in Great Britain by
HarperCollins Manufacturing, Glasgow

EDDIE AND THE SWINE FAMILY

Many children's stories begin with "Once upon a time". This one, however, starts with the words "Once upon a Swine" because this is a book about a pig called Eddie and his family, the Swines. Eddie is the youngest in the family. Helpful and very friendly, he is a credit to pigs everywhere, which is more than can be said for the rest of the tribe:

Alistair and Alfred

Eddie's twin brothers, and they are the meanest, greediest porkers you're ever likely to meet.

Alistair and Alfred have two loves in their lives.

The first is themselves,

the second is food.

They live to eat and no one, but no one, stands between them and their passion for grub! These horrible hogs will stop at nothing to get food. They even *sold* their own grandmother

for a slap-up meal at the top restaurant, "Piggeries". Luckily, a week

later, she was duly rescued by
Eddie: he found her doing the
washing-up in the restaurant kitchen!

These portly porkers have no hearts
– gluttony is their middle name.

(As I mentioned before, Alistair and
Alfred's first love is themselves, and
they did in fact want this story to
start with the words: "Once upon an
Alistair and Alfred", but when it was
pointed out that it didn't have quite
the same ring as "Once upon a
Swine" they decided to settle for that
instead – but not without the firm
warning that if I forgot to put it in
they'd move in with me, eat the
contents of my fridge (not to
mention my dustbin) and lounge

about all day watching cooking programmes on TV! Of course, under those conditions I had no choice but to agree. Well, what would you have done?!)

The twins take great pride in their appearance, modelling themselves on those infamous gangsters of the 1920s "Hog Capone" and "Piglet Face Maloney".

 Dressing themselves in high class suits, they're rarely seen without their trilbies and dark glasses.

Alistair and Alfred – together they're the heaviest burden of Eddie's life, but by no means the only one...

Winifred

The only girl in the family. Winifred is very spoilt. She is incredibly big-headed and her only ambition in life is to star in a soap opera, preferably the one about the everyday goings-on in a hospital.

Winifred dreams of being Nurse Pinky, The Kindest Nurse in the World, whose kindness and dedication goes unnoticed by Doctor

Swill, The Most Overworked Doctor
in the World. Winifred longs for one
thing only and that particular thing
is **FAME!**

Mr and Mrs Swine

Doris and
Dennis Swine
– ballroom
dancing
champions
extraordinaire.
From the foxtrot to
the rumba, they're
the champs.

The living room is crammed full of
the trophies they've won. From
Cleethorpes to Chicago, Doris and
Dennis have twirled the boards in
dance halls everywhere.

So great is their passion for dancing that one moment Mrs Swine might be clearing the kitchen table and the next – WHOOSH! she's whipped off the tablecloth, scattered plates and cutlery everywhere, wrapped the cloth round herself and started prancing about the kitchen doing the lambada! And heaven help the postman, milkman or paperboy if they happen to be near the front door, because Mrs Swine will have them waltzing up the path more quickly than you can say "olé!"

Or Mr Swine could be quite happily

pruning his roses when suddenly he's rammed a rose between his teeth and is doing a tango with the electric lawnmower up and down the drive!

Doris and Dennis will dance at any time, in any place and anywhere. This means they're away quite a lot, leaving Eddie in charge.

Eddie

He may be the youngest and the smallest pig in the family, but little Eddie has more intelligence in one of his trotters than Alistair, Alfred or Winifred has in the whole of their rather large bodies. Mrs Swine calls Eddie her "Little Swinestein" (after Albert Swinestein, the great pig physicist and mathematician) and

insists to her fellow ballroom dancers that her Eddie will go to university and become a great scientist or maybe even an astropig. (The first pig in space!) Eddie finds this very embarrassing.

The Swine family:

Greedy pigs
Alistair and Alfred,

star-struck,
pampered
piggy Winifred

13

and Doris and Dennis — so wrapped
up in *slow, slow, quick, quick, slow*
that they tend to forget about their
little darlings.

And without Eddie, their other little
darlings would be even more of a
problem...

CHAPTER ONE

Once upon a Swine, (I remembered!) the day dawned bright and clear over No. 34 Stye Close. The neighbours had risen early. They knew that Alistair and Alfred would soon be on the scrounge, pinching milk from the doorsteps. But this particular morning they needn't have bothered, because the terrible twins

had bigger things on their minds!
They were holed up in their bedroom,
planning and plotting the next move
in their biggest venture yet.

Alistair was studying the local
newspaper closely. In his purple
polka dot pyjamas he turned the
pages slowly then, with a thick
black felt-tip pen, he drew a large
circle on the page.

"This is it, Alfred!" he shouted. "This is the one!"

Alfred grabbed the paper from him and held it right up to his snout (he was very shortsighted). Slowly (he couldn't read too well either!) he read the item out loud.

" 'Grand opening'," he read. " 'Grand opening today of Pedro's Pasta Pizza Place to be opened by Doctor Swill, star of the hit TV series, "Heartache Hospital". Dr Swill will be appearing at 2.00 p.m. Bring the family! There's fun for all – and the world's largest——' " Here Alfred stopped, his mouth and eyes open wide.

"Go on!" said Alistair excitedly.

"The world's largest...

"PIZZA!" Alfred exclaimed.

"That's right," said Alistair. "We're talking big here, Alfred. Megabig. Just imagine a pizza so huge that not even WE could manage to eat it all at once, not even *us*."

Alfred looked at Alistair, his eyes nearly as big as a pizza pan.

"Yeah," was all he could say. "Yeah."

"The only problem," continued Alistair, "is pinching the blooming thing, but as usual, Alfred, your brainy brother has come up with a brilliant plan. Now, come over here and I'll whisper what it is."

* * *

Eddie, Winifred and Mr and Mrs Swine were downstairs in the kitchen.

"Where are the terrible two?" remarked Mr Swine. "Funny that they're not down here for breakfast."

"Oh, you know those boys, they need their beauty sleep," said Mrs Swine proudly. She was busy putting the finishing touches to yet another dancing dress. This one was a rather sickly lime green, covered in bright pink sequins.

"Is your suit pressed and are your shoes cleaned?" she asked "You know the coach leaves at one o'clock sharp."

Mr and Mrs Swine were entering yet another dancing competition that afternoon. Normally they told everyone where they were dancing, but for some reason they had been particularly secretive about this one.

"Yes, Doris," said Mr Swine, eating his breakfast.

"And you won't be needing that," Mrs Swine whisked his breakfast away from him. "You know a heavy breakfast plays havoc with your

Military Two Step. Now, hurry
upstairs and get yourself ready! Give
Alistair and Alfred a call too. It's
time they came down for breakfast."

Mr Swine went upstairs obediently.

"Mumsy?" whined Winifred.

"Yes, sweetums?" answered Mrs
Swine.

"Mumsy, may I borrow your purple
dress? You know, the one with the

roses sewn all over it?"

"You most certainly may not,
Winifred," said Mrs Swine sternly.
"That's my most expensive dress,
and it's also one of my prize-
winning lucky ones."

"But I want it!" squealed Winifred,
stamping her trotters and hurling her
cereal spoon across the room. "Want
it! Want it! Want it!"

"Now, Winifred, sweety, stop that,"
said Mrs Swine. "You're not
borrowing it, and that's final."

Winifred stood up and flounced out
of the kitchen.

"That's what
you think,
Mumsy dearest,"
she whispered
under her breath.
Winifred had other ideas. She, too,
had seen the local newspaper and
intended to go to see Dr Swill open
Pedro's Pasta Pizza Place. This was
her big chance to break into acting
and, possibly, dream of dreams,
SOAP OPERAS!

Mrs Swine went upstairs too, to finish doing her face.

As usual, Eddie was left with the washing-up to do.   Pulling on a pair of trotter-shaped rubber gloves,  he set to work on the mountain of crockery, trying to imagine what it must be like to live with a normal family.

Suddenly, there was a loud rumble from upstairs, followed by a banging noise and then a thud. Eddie knew it was just Alistair and Alfred coming downstairs.

"How's tricks, Ed?" said Alistair,

slapping him on the back and
grabbing some leftover toast and
half a fried egg from a plate.

"OK," replied Eddie, up to his elbows
in scummy washing-up water. "You
both look particularly smart today."

Alfred did a twirl and fingered the
lapel of his suit carefully. "New suits,
special day," he said proudly.

"What's
the special
day, then?"
asked
Eddie.

"That's *our* secret," snapped Alistair.

"Mind your own business, baby brother. Come along, Alfred," he said snootily. "We've work to do."

Eddie knew the troublesome two were up to something – and if they went off without having breakfast, that something *had* to be serious!

It was midday, and Winifred was up to no good. She had taken her mother's prize-winning purple dress from the wardrobe, and was now admiring

herself in her bedroom mirror. She
squealed excitedly and clapped her
trotters together at the sight of
herself in her mother's dress, which
was at least a size too small. She
was also wearing a pair of Mrs
Swine's dancing shoes, red and
glittery, with pin-thin spiky three-
inch heels. They were pinching her
trotters, but
Winifred knew she
had to suffer in the
name of beauty!
Perched on top of her
head was a huge wig.
It was backcombed and stood
at least a foot high, and her little
pink ears stuck out on either side.

Winifred studied herself in the mirror

for a long time, adjusting the wig slightly. Then she applied some of her mother's lipstick and stood back again to admire the finished result. Being a pig of very little taste, she decided she looked absolutley beautiful. And Winifred, also an incredibly big-headed little madam, was sure that if Dr Swill, star of "Heartache Hospital", was to set eyes on her, he would instantly see her great beauty and obvious talent and insist that she become his leading lady and take over the role of Nurse Pinky, The Kindest Nurse in the World!

"I *will* be a star," Winifred said out loud. "I will! I will! I will!" she repeated crossly, stamping up and

down. She wobbled dangerously in
the glittery shoes.

CHAPTER TWO

Meanwhile, in the High Street, a large crowd had gathered to watch the huge crane which was to lower the gigantic pizza through the glass roof of Pedro's Pasta Pizza Place. There it was to be displayed in all its glory before being cut up and shared amongst the crowd. No one knew how Mr Pedro was going to get the pizza into his oven!

Men wearing donkey jackets and bright yellow hard hats were standing at the bottom of the crane, looking up and shouting, "Hold it! Hold it!" and "Steady! Steady!" as the arm of the crane swung gently from side to side.

Out of sight, behind a wall, were Alistair and Alfred, eyeing the preparations with excited glee.

"It's going to be big, Alfie," said Alistair.

"It's going to be as big as a house," declared Alfred.

"Right," said Alistair. "Now we've seen the layout, this is the plan. That Dr Swill bloke is making an appearance at two o'clock, right?"

"Right," said Alfred, checking his Mickey Mouse watch intently, though he couldn't actually tell the time!

"So just after he gets out of the car," continued Alistair, "we move forward and grab him, shove him in the back of the van and drive off. Then we hold him to ransom until they deliver the pizza to us."

"But how will Mr Pedro know where to send the pizza?" asked Alfred, looking puzzled. "If we rush off, no one will know who we are, or where we're going."

Alistair shook his head and sighed, "I'll tell you what, Alfred," he said very sarcastically, "we'll tell him, shall we? We'll go up to Mr Pedro and say – 'Hello, Mr Pedro, we're Alistair and Alfred Swine and we want your pizza, so we're going to kidnap that top Doc celebrity Dr Swill who's opening your restaurant today, and we'll be taking him to

No. 34 Stye Close – oh, that's where we live, by the way!' Don't be so stupid, Alfred!" And he pinched his snout

"We'll pin a ransom note to the pizza, you daft boy," he explained. "That way they won't know who we are, but they will know what we want. I've already made the note."

And from his pocket he proudly produced a grubby piece of paper with newspaper letters stuck on.

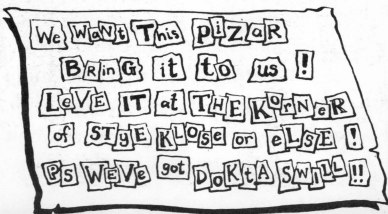

We WaNt This PIZaR
BRinG it to us !
LeVe IT at THE KoRneR
of STyE KLoSe or eLSE !
Ps WeVe got DoKtA SWiLL !!

"Cor!" said Alfred. "It's just like the films."

"Right," said Alistair, proudly. "There's nothing much doing here at the moment, so let's go and get some food."

Back at the house, Eddie had finally finished the washing-up.

He decided he would spend the afternoon at the park with some of his friends. He was a popular pig – as popular as his brothers were unpopular! Those who knew the other Swines thought that Mrs Swine 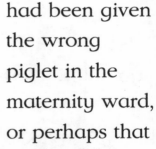 had been given the wrong piglet in the maternity ward, or perhaps that he was adopted, because he was so different from the rest of the Swines. Not only did he not think about food all the time, he was also usually the one to rescue his brothers and sister from whatever trouble they got themselves into.

He went upstairs to change into his brand new baseball jacket. He knew that Mr and Mrs Swine had already left to meet the coach that was to take them to the championships, but as he passed Winifred's room he saw her preening herself in the mirror.

"Hey, Winifred!" said Eddie. "You've got Mum's best dress on! She said you couldn't borrow it!"

"Oh, shut up!" sneered Winifred.

"She'll never know. Don't you dare tell her, you little creep. Anyway, it looks miles better on me. Now kindly get out of my room, I'm busy."

"You don't look very busy," said Eddie, studying Winifred's remarkable wig at a safe distance. "You just look stupid. Why are you all dressed up, anyway? It's Saturday afternoon."

"Because," said Winifred, pausing for effect, "I'm going to appear on film. Haven't you seen the paper?" And she threw it across the room at Eddie. He picked it up and read the advertisement about the grand opening.

"But, Winifred, don't you realize how many people will be there?" said Eddie.

"Yes, but don't you see, Eddie? There's no way that Dr Swill could fail to notice me when I look like this!" Winifred waltzed round the room, teetering on her stilettos.

"You can say that again," muttered Eddie. "But anyway," he added, more loudly, "where have Alistair and Alfred gone today?"

He was beginning to have his suspicions, for he had seen the words LARGEST and PIZZA written in the advertisement. He knew that anything big and edible was bound to attract the porky pair.

"How would I know?" scoffed
Winifred. "I don't know, and I don't
care." She disliked her brothers
intensely. She
would far rather
have had a little
sister, so that she
could boss her
around and pull
her hair and get
her to run errands
all over the place!

"I must be going if I'm to be in time
for my debut," she continued
haughtily. "Are you coming, Eddie,
or are you going to meet your
horrid common friends?"

"Well," said Eddie, seeing that Winifred was *very* determined, "I *was* going to go to the park, but I think I'd better come with you."

"Chop, chop, then," said Winifred, sharply.

"Shall we take my bike?" suggested Eddie. "It'll be quicker."

Winifred looked horrified. "Certainly not!" she gasped. "Whatever would it look like, ME, Winifred Swine, budding starlet, turning up on the back of a pushbike? I have my reputation to consider, you know!" And she swept out of the room, snout in the air.

CHAPTER THREE

The gigantic pizza was ready,
hanging from the crane like some
huge flying saucer. It was waiting
to be lowered into Mr Pedro's
restaurant. Some of the cheese had
begun to ooze over the edge.

Attached to its side was a grubby,
dog-eared piece of paper, which

fluttered in the breeze. It was the twins' ransom note. They had pinned it on when the workmen had gone to lunch.

(It had taken all the willpower Alistair and Alfred could muster to walk away from the pizza without taking several massive bites out of it. They had hurried off to the chip shop instead!)

Now they were standing at the front of the restaurant, just by the entrance. A large number of people was gathering behind them, getting quite excited about the expected arrival of Dr Swill. One small boy in particular was pushing and shoving against Alfred's legs.

"Oi, fatty!" he said to Alfred, pushing at him again and again. "Shove out the way, will yer? I can't see!"

Alfred turned round and picked him up by his shirt collar, so he could see eye to eye with the little shrimp.

"Look, sonny," he said. "You're beginning to get on my nerves." As Alfred glared at him, the little boy grinned nervously, recognising the face of the most feared sweet-stealer in town.

"Sorry, mister," he said sheepishly.

"Sorry?" said Alfred. "Sorry's not good enough. Got any sweets, any food?"

And with that he turned the child upside down and shook him, so that lollipops, chews and a packet of crisps fell out of his pockets and onto the pavement. Alistair heard the noise, and turned round.

"Put the kid down, Alfred, for goodness' sake," he said, peering at the red-faced boy over the top of his sunglasses. "We don't want to draw attention to ourselves."

Alfred put him down carelessly, and the boy quickly disappeared into another part of the crowd, leaving, like the wise child he was, his sweets and crisps for Alfred.

Suddenly, a large sleek limousine glided slowly up to the entrance.

"It's him! It's him!" shouted somebody in the crowd as the door of the car opened and the tall lanky figure of Dr Swill emerged. He was wearing the white coat that he always wore in the TV series, and round his neck hung a stethoscope, just in case no one recognized him off the screen!

"Dr Swill, cooee! Over here!" a squeaky voice called from the crowd. Dr Swill looked across, but all he could see was an enormous blonde wig bobbing up and down. He flashed a pearly white smile to the crowd.

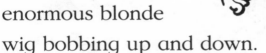

"Cooee, Dr Swill! Cooee!"

The wig was following him, still bobbing up and down. But now a little pink trotter could be seen waving frantically in a sea of faces.

Dr Swill was within a few feet of Alistair and Alfred. Suddenly he felt himself being lifted off the ground by the two largest pigs he had ever seen. And they were both wearing sunglasses!

"I say..." he spluttered, his feet and legs pedalling up and down as if he were riding a bicycle.

"Move aside, ladies and gentlemen,"
announced Alistair.
"Dr Swill is needed urgently
elsewhere – he has to perform an
immediate operation."

"But I'm not a REAL doctor!" protested
Dr Swill. "I'm an *actor*, you fool!"

"Yes, yes," said Alistair hurriedly,
and they bundled him into their van.
As Alistair and Alfred climbed into
the front, there was a loud thud on
the roof and everything inside the
van went dark. Dr Swill screamed
as the back doors suddenly opened
and the enormous wig he'd spotted
earlier climbed in after him.

"Why, Dr Swill," said a breathless

voice as Alfred skidded off up the road. "What a romantic way to meet!" And the TV doctor felt two porky arms wrap themselves round him. Winifred had got him!

* * *

It was chaos back at Pedro's Pasta Pizza Place.

The crowd were getting angry. They'd come to see the famous Dr Swill and to get a free slice of pizza. So far they weren't getting either. Dr Swill had disappeared, and so had the giant pizza!

Mr Pedro was very upset. He was wailing, "My pizza! My pizza!" at the top of his voice and looking skywards towards the empty crane.

Two policemen were doing their best to calm him.

"Now, sir, tell us exactly what happened," one of them said in a serious voice. Mr Pedro just spluttered into his handkerchief.

"Do-You-Speak-English?" the other policemen asked slowly.

"Of course I speak English," snapped Mr Pedro. "I'm no more Italian than you are. My name's Ron Brown, and I come from Watford!"

"Very well, sir," coughed the policeman nervously. "Then would you kindly tell us what you saw?"

"It all happened so quickly," explained Mr Pedro-Brown, blowing his nose loudly. "One minute the pizza was hanging over my restaurant, and the next I knew, that crane had swung round and my pizza, my beautiful, beautiful pizza, was flying through the air."

"Did you see where it landed, sir?" asked the policeman, writing

Saturday ~ 20 past 2.
Englishman posing as an Italian.
Flying Pizza.

in his notebook.

"It landed on top of some grubby van, driven by two very sinister-looking pigs."

* * *

Alistair and Alfred were now speeding up the High Street and away from the chaos. Alfred was hunched over the steering wheel, his snout pressed up against the windscreen. The wipers were moving backwards and forwards frantically,

trying to clear pizza off the screen.
Melted cheese was oozing
everywhere and black olives and
mushy tomatoes were flying in all
directions, splattering astonished
passers-by.

"I can't see," said Alfred crossly.
"The window's gone all cheesy."

"It's the pizza, Alfred," shouted
Alistair above the squeak and swish

of the windscreen wipers. "It's gone and landed on top of the van!"

"Cor, great!" said Alfred, delightedly. "Meals on wheels," and he wound down his window, put out a trotter and grabbed himself a piece of pizza from the roof. The van swerved dangerously from side to side as Alfred tried to steer with one trotter and eat with the other. Dr Swill screamed hysterically from the back.

"What's happening?" he blubbered. "Why have I been abducted in this manner? I'm a famous actor, you know! Half the country's police force will be looking for me by now."

"Oh, don't be so dramatic," said Alistair, munching on his piece of pizza. "We only wanted the pizza, not you, and besides, you're not THAT famous anyway. We don't need you any more – you might as well get out!"

"He is famous! He is! He is!" squealed Winifred from the back. "And I wanted to appear on film with him, and now you've spoilt everything. I hate you both! Hate, hate, hate you!"

"Shut up, Winifred," snapped Alfred. "We're not exactly in love with you, either. What are you doing here, anyway? This was our plan, and we don't want any cissy stupid girls in on it."

"Well, I'm here now," snorted Winifred. "And it's a good job, too. Dr Swill needs me and I'm not going anywhere until I'm seen on film with him. I've waited years for this chance and I'm not about to give up my big break into stardom because of two ignoramuses like you. So keep on driving till we reach the Television Studios.
Dr Swill and I are going to take a screen test together!"

"Television studios? Screen test?" laughed Dr Swill. "My dear girl, whatever do you mean?"

"Dr Swill," said Winifred sternly. "It's quite simple. I want the part of Nurse Pinky, The Kindest Nurse in the World, and I intend to get it. You see I'm VERY, VERY talented, but I have to blossom."

"But this is preposterous!" exclaimed Dr Swill. "I'm an actor, not a casting director. Now, let me out of this van and we'll say no more about it. You're all quite mad!"

"No!" said Winifred adamantly. "Alfred, turn this van round! Take us to the studios."

"You must be joking," said Alistair.

"We're taking this pizza to Fred the Fridge's freezer warehouse, just till the heat's off us. Then we can tuck in."

"But what about me?" gasped Dr Swill, having visions of being locked in a gigantic icebox with the pizza.

Alistair turned round and peered at him over the top of his dark glasses. "Well, if you can hang on until me and my brother have sorted our affairs out, we'll drop you off at the bus stop, OK?"

"You're not going anywhere, Alistair." Winifred stamped her trotters. "Except to the TV studios, that is. Because if you don't, I'm going to tell Mumsy about the time you sold Grandma and..."

"OK, OK," interrupted Alistair, "enough, enough. Alfred, turn this van round! We're going to take this sneaky sister of ours to the TV studios."

* * *

Meanwhile, Eddie was trying to calm Mr Pedro, alias Mr Brown from Watford, owner of Pedro's Pasta Pizza Place. Only this place was minus a pizza. Eddie explained that the disappearance of Dr Swill by Alistair and Alfred had been no more than a practical joke.

"Oh, blow him," said Mr Pedro-Brown waving his handkerchief around. "I wanted Nurse Pinky, but she's presenting the prize at some dancing competition today, so I had to have Swill instead, and very expensive he was too. No, it's my pizza, I WANT IT BACK!"

"Well," said Eddie, thoughtfully, "I understand that pizza somehow landed on top of my brother's van, but that's hardly their fault, is it?"

But Eddie knew whose fault it really was. Winifred's...

When Winifred saw that her beloved Dr Swill was about to be whisked from under her very snout by her beastly brothers, she had hobbled in her high heels to the crane and tried to catch Dr Swill on the end of the crane's big hook, where he would have dangled in mid-air and been completely under her command. But she had pulled the wrong lever on the crane and sent the pizza flying through the air till it landed –

splat! – on top of the van.

Winifred's plan had backfired and now she and the giant pizza were trundling up the road. But at least she had Dr Swill, her passport to fame and her stepping stone to stardom!

"Now, Mr Pedro-Brown," said Eddie, "I will endeavour to get your pizza back. Please excuse my brothers' behaviour – their sense of humour can be a little extreme at times, but give me a few hours and I'll get it returned to you, somehow."

"Well," said Mr Pedro-Brown, thoughtfully. "I *would* rather it were returned without any fuss. This sort of scandal could be bad for business. Where do you think they've gone?"

"I think," said Eddie, getting on his pushbike, "that they might well be heading to the television studios."

Eddie knew his Winifred. He was pretty certain that if Winifred were with them, the lure of fame and Dr Swill, together with Winifred threatening to throw a tantrum, meant that the brothers had to be going that way.

* * *

Alfred had got lost again. His sense
of direction was appalling, and he
couldn't see much further
than the end of his short
snout, even when
there wasn't pizza
on the windscreen.

He'd driven the wrong
way up a one way
street – twice! Three
times round a
roundabout – the
wrong way! And he was now
heading towards the M1.

"Go left! Go left!" shouted Alistair,

pulling the steering wheel away from him. The tyres on the van screeched, and so did Dr Swill!

Up ahead a sign could be seen. In big bold letters it read:

A.B.C.
TELEVISION STUDIOS.
ALL VISITORS MUST REPORT TO THE OFFICE.

"Slow down, Alfred!" said Alistair, adjusting his tie and straightening his hat.

As they approached the entrance, a
barrier came down to stop them
going any further. A man dressed in
a bright blue uniform stepped
forward from a sentry box and
tapped briskly on the side window.
He had some difficulty finding a
piece of glass without any melted
cheese on it.

Alistair stared coldly at him through
his dark glasses. TAP, TAP, TAP!
The guard tapped harder and
scowled back. Alistair wound his
window down slowly.

"Yes?" he asked drily.

"Excuse me, er, sir," said the security
guard, poking his head through the

window. "Do you 'ave a pass?"

"Pass?" said Alistair. "A pass? Take a look in the back and you'll see that we have a very important passenger. We don't need a pass!"

The security guard peered closer. "Why, it's Dr Swill!" he said in amazement.

"Yes, but..." spluttered Dr Swill.

Winifred pinched him hard.

"Yes, my good man," she interrupted. "And I'M the new star of 'Heartache Hospital', so kindly let us enter."

The guard looked at her and then back at Alistair.

"Hmm," he hesitated. "That's as may be, but what's this mess on top of your vehicle?"

"Mess, mate?" said Alfred, leaning over and glaring at the guard. "That's no mess, that's a pizza and it's ours, so keep your hands off!" Alistair kicked him on the ankle.

"What my dear brother means is that the pizza is there for advertising purposes. You see, Dr Swill opened a pizza parlour earlier today, and we're displaying that fact by driving the good doctor with the pizza to the television studios."

"I see," said the guard, looking impressed. "Promotion stuff, eh?"

He leaned forward and whispered to Alistair, "Goodness knows, he needs it. His ratings have dropped dramatically lately," and he nodded knowingly at Alistair, who nodded back.
The guard stepped away from the van and lifted the barrier,
"Off you go, then!" he shouted, waving his hand.

CHAPTER FOUR

Eddie meanwhile was heading in the right direction. He knew he had to get to the twins before Mr Pedro-Brown or the police. Somehow he had to pacify poor Dr Swill, or who knew what trouble he could cause.

"This," he thought, "is the last time I help Alistair and Alfred out. They've really gone and done it this time, stealing *and* kidnapping."

* * *

"Pull in here," said Alistair, pointing to a space in the forecourt.

Alfred parked the van – badly.

"Right. Out you get, Dr Swill," said Alistair. "You obviously know this place, so show us the way in, and no funny business. We don't want to draw attention to ourselves."

Dr Swill was very relieved to be out of the smelly old van, but wished that the dreadful pig in a wig would let go of his arm.

"I can almost hear the roar of the crowd," gasped Winifred. "Just imagine, Dr Swill, you and I immortalised for ever on the screen!" And she sighed deeply, wiping away an imaginary tear.

Dr Swill was filled with absolute horror at the thought of acting alongside this mentally deranged pig. He had come to the conclusion that all three of them had escaped from some sort of pigs' asylum, were quite mad, and were extremely dangerous! So Dr Swill, being a coward, had decided against any heroics and thought he'd better play along with them until he could safely make his escape.

It could only give a much-needed boost to his popularity when the public found out about his ordeal at the hands of three depraved pigs.

He could see the headline now:

TV DOC IN CRAZED PIGS SHOCK!!!

That should bring the fans back in their hundreds!

Dr Swill led the way in through the back entrance. The pigs and he found themselves in a long corridor facing two large double doors.

A notice read:

FINALS OF THE
"COME PRANCING"
BALLROOM DANCING
CHAMPIONSHIPS.
COMPETITORS ONLY.

"This must be what Mum and Dad are in," said Alfred. "It must be the event they were being so secretive about."

"They never told us they were going to be on television," said Winifred sulkily.

As she spoke, they all heard from behind them the sound of approaching footsteps.

"Quick!" said Alistair, opening the double doors. "In here!" And he pushed Dr Swill and Winifred through. Alfred followed noisily.

They found themselves in a huge hall, the size of an aeroplane hangar. From the middle of the ceiling hung an enormous sparkly ball spinning round and round. The dance floor was a riot of colour, with ladies swamped in oceans of

multicoloured net on which
thousands of sequins sparkled like
diamonds. Winifred gasped as she
spotted the television cameras at the
end of the dance floor.

"Do you think there's any food?" asked Alfred, looking round hopefully.

"Sssh," said Alistair, as a small man carrying a clipboard hurried towards them. "Here comes some nosy-looking bloke."

It was the floor manager.

"You're a bit late," he said sharply. "But never mind. Now, who's dancing with who? Mmm—" he said, looking at Alistair and Alfred. "Two males together, good, good, variety, that's what's needed. Like the suits, boys. But the glasses will *have* to go."

Alistair and Alfred gave him one of their famous glares over the tops of their sunglasses, and the little man coughed nervously. He quickly turned his attention to Dr Swill and Winifred, who was still clutching Dr Swill's arm.

"Nice dress, dear," he said to Winifred approvingly. "Is that your real hair?" He fingered the wig cautiously. "No, I thought not. Oh dear."

He looked at Dr Swill dressed in his white coat with the stethoscope still hanging round his neck. "You're *supposed* to wear black tie and tails," he sighed, flicking the stethoscope so it hit Dr Swill on the end of his nose. "And jewellery of this size is *not* allowed! But never mind, there's no time to change now."

"But I'm..." Dr Swill began to protest.

"Pin these on your backs," said the floor manager, handing out cardboard numbers to each of them before hurrying off.

"I'm getting out of here," said Alfred, turning on his heels and making for the door. "I'm not dancing for

anyone, its bad for my image and
I'll scuff my shoes as well!"

"Look," said Alistair, pulling Alfred
back by his shirt collar, "there's no
way we can go back outside now.
We'll stay here a while, Alfie," he
whispered. "Just till the coast is
clear. Then we'll leave Winifred and
scarper with the pizza. Besides,
there's a buffet table over there in
the corner, and it's absolutely
heaped with food."

Alfred followed Alistair's pointing
trotter and spied a long trestle table
covered with enormous quantities of
sandwiches and rolls, crisps, peanuts

and other delights. In the middle
was a large three-tiered chocolate
and cream gateau. Alfred licked his
lips and nodded. "OK," was all he
said.

Suddenly the lights around them
went down and changed to a deep
red.

"Ladies and gentlemen," a voice
boomed over the loudspeaker.
"Welcome to the finals of the 'Come
Prancing' ballroom dancing
championships. We're going to start
the show off with the cha cha, so
could all the contestants take their
partners and proceed to the dance
floor. When I say 'Action!', the
cameras will start rolling and you'll

be seen on millions of TV screens up and down the country. So take your positions, ladies and gentlemen, please."

Winifred had stars in her eyes. Millions would be watching her. She made straight to the middle of the dance floor, pulling the bewildered Dr Swill along behind her.

"Excuse me! Excuse me!" Winifred pushed the other contestants aside.

"Winifred!" There was a shrill cry from one of them. "Whatever do you think your playing at? Put that poor doctor down!"

It was Doris Swine, Winifred's mother, already in position for the cha cha.

"No!" said Winifred rudely.

"We'll deal with you later, you naughty girl," said Mr Swine crossly as the director gave the order for the cameras to start filming.

All the contestants were in position and looked as if they were frozen in time, standing cheek to cheek with arms outstretched.

The music started. Suddenly the whole hall came alive as everyone started to move in one direction across the floor to the beat of the music.

Everyone, that is, except for Winifred. She was moving in the opposite direction towards the television cameras. Dr Swill was trying to escape her clutches.

"That's it," he hissed, trying desperately to push Winifred away. "I've had enough! This is all too humiliating! I don't know why I let myself get this far."

"No, no, Dr Swill!" exclaimed Winifred, edging towards the TV camera. "This is my big moment to break into television!"

"Never mind BREAK INTO television," snapped Dr Swill, "you'll probably BREAK EVERY television set up and down the country!"

Winifred ignored him and stood in front of one of the cameras. The man behind it motioned to her to move. Winifred thought he wanted her to move closer. She pouted at the camera and blinked her eyelids. The cameraman waved his arm frantically at her again, and once again Winifred moved closer.

She was no more than a foot away from the camera and she thrust her face right up to it and very nearly kissed the lens!

The cameraman screamed and leapt backwards. "Get out of the way," he hissed. "It's dancing the viewers want to see, not some horrible close-up of a pig's snout."

"That's where you're wrong," said Winifred. "This man here," and she pushed Dr Swill in front of her, "is famous, and I, too, will jolly well soon be. So just keep that camera focused on me or I'll get my brothers on to you."

"I'll do no such thing," said the cameraman, and began to wheel the camera away to another part of the floor.

Meanwhile the cha cha had come to an end, and the contestants had begun to do a dance called the tango.

Winifred continued to follow one of the cameras round the floor. If it

went to the left, so would Winifred.
If it went to the right, Winifred
would too. Backwards and forwards,
from side to side, danced Winifred
and the helpless Dr Swill. He had
given up all hope of ever
disengaging himself from this
horrendous hog and her two beastly
brothers.

He'd noticed that Alistair and Alfred
were still hanging round the edge of
the dance floor, looking suitably
sinister. They had also been joined
by a short little pig wearing a
baseball cap.

"That little runt is probably one of
their sidekicks," thought Dr Swill,
and he decided it was best not to

attempt his escape just yet. Maybe the little one was a judo expert, or some sort of martial arts fanatic, he thought. They were usually on the small side.

So he continued to tango with Winifred and consider his future, and dreamed of emigrating as they followed the camera round and round the hall.

CHAPTER FIVE

The "little runt" was, as you may
have guessed, Eddie, and he had
come to try to help Dr Swill as well
as return the pizza to its rightful
owner, Mr Pedro-Brown.

"Look," said Eddie, crossly, glaring
at Alistair and Alfred each in turn,
"you two are in a right mess, you
stole that pizza and, worse than that,
much worse, you stole Dr Swill!"

"Oh, shut up moaning, Eddie," said Alistair. "He looks as though he's enjoying himself, doesn't he?" Alistair and Alfred sniggered as they saw Dr Swill lifted high into the air by Winifred and spun round above her head as she teetered round and round in a circle. She was trying desperately to get noticed. The other contestants were furious.

The cameras were trying their best to dodge Winifred, but every now and then she would manage to get herself on their screens. And millions of viewers up and down the country were banging the tops of their television sets, convinced that theirs were on the blink when what appeared to be a large pink blob would take up the whole of the screen! Finally, to great applause round the hall, the dancing came to an end. Winifred was loving it, bowing and kissing to the crowd. Dr Swill stood at her side, stunned and still reeling from the shock of being manhandled by this wretched pig.

Then it was announced over the loudspeaker that Nurse Pinky, star of Heartache Hospital, was to come forward to present the prize to the winners. Nurse Pinky stepped out onto the dance floor to great applause. She was swathed in yards of emerald green silk, and draped round her neck was a softer-than-soft floaty pink feather boa. Nurse

Pinky walked elegantly across the floor, glancing this way and that, with the merest hint of a smile on her lips as the cameras eagerly followed her on either side.

Winifred of course was fuming, and by the time Nurse Pinky had reached the centre of the dance floor she was positively seething.

"It is my great pleasure," squeaked

Nurse Pinky in a high-pitched voice, "to present this cup." She held up a large, gleaming, silver cup towards the cameras and flashed a pearly white smile, "To the winners of this year's 'Come Prancing' competition. They are..." She paused to open a little gold envelope, then announced breathlessly, "Doris and Dennis Swine!"

Watching a beaming Mr and Mrs Swine stepping forward to rapturous applause was more than Winifred could bear. She rushed forward and pushed Nurse Pinky aside, "Move it, skinny!" she snapped. "You look like a mouldy stick of rock in that dress!"

"I beg your pardon?" gasped Nurse Pinky.

"You heard, beanpole," sneered Winifred. "Now, give me that cup!" and she snatched it away from a startled Nurse Pinky.

"Winifred, how dare you behave in this manner!" said Mrs Swine crossly. "We won that cup, not you! Give it back this instant!"

"Shan't! Shan't! Shan't!" squealed
Winifred, stamping her trotters.
"This cup belongs to me and Dr
Swill, by rights."

Nurse Pinky
stepped
forward,

"Why, Dr Swill!"
she exclaimed.
"Whatever
are you doing here?"

"I can explain," began Dr Swill, but
at that moment chaos descended.
Winifred grabbed the end of Nurse
Pinky's feather boa, and Nurse Pinky
grabbed the top of Winifred's wig
and promptly pulled it off!

Mr Swine grabbed the cup. Alistair
and Alfred, who were stuffing their
fat faces, thought they'd join in by
throwing soggy egg sandwiches and
cream-filled meringues at the
flabbergasted contestants.

SPLAT! A gooey meringue splattered
into someone's face.

SPLODGE! A soggy
cheese and tomato roll was
squashed onto someone's back.

Winifred and Nurse Pinky were still pulling and pushing. Winifred, much the larger of the two, gave one almighty shove, sending Nurse Pinky flying face first into the chocolate gateau!

"Oh dear," said Eddie, as he helped a wailing Nurse Pinky onto a nearby chair. Her face was covered in thick dark chocolate and there was a glacé cherry stuck on the end of her nose.

"You two had better get out of here," he said to Alistair and Alfred.

"But the fun's just starting!" replied Alistair. And with one movement he pulled the cherry off Nurse Pinky's nose and popped it into his mouth!

Nurse Pinky wailed louder.

"On second thoughts," shouted Alistair, putting his trotters over his ears. "Maybe we should. Come on, Alfred, let's go."

Alfred looked longingly at the buffet table as Alistair marched over and started pulling a kicking and screaming Winifred towards the exit door. Dr Swill, now out of Winifred's vice-like grip, rushed over to assist his co-star of Heartache Hospital.

"Look at the trouble you've caused!" raged Dr Swill at Eddie.

"I'm very sorry," said Eddie apologetically. "But there's no real harm done, is there?"

"That's as may be," replied Dr Swill crossly, though he was taken aback by Eddie's friendly and apologetic manner. "But Nurse Pinky and I have been through a terrible ordeal."

Nurse Pinky wailed louder still and nodded in agreement.

"That horrible pig!" she blubbered. "That horrible, horrible pig!"

Dr Swill patted her shoulder lightly.

"I know, I know," he said sympathetically, and shuddered as he thought of Winifred and their display upon the dance floor.

"But, you see," said Eddie, trying hard to explain. "My sister Winifred was desperate to appear on film with you, Dr Swill. She really is a big fan of yours, you know."

Dr Swill looked very smug. "Well," he said proudly, "when you're as famous as I am, I suppose you must expect hysterical young girls, not to mention pigs, throwing themselves at you. It's one of the drawbacks of being famous and handsome, of course," he added, smirking and looking even more pleased with himself. And Eddie nodded in agreement, knowing that Dr Swill, being the big-headed actor that he was, would take the matter no further. He wouldn't want any bad publicity.

"But what about me?" sniffed Nurse Pinky indignantly. "That dreadful pig has ruined my reputation. You see," she looked at Eddie and fluttered her eyelashes, "I play Nurse Pinky, The Kindest Nurse in the World, and I really have to live up to that image."

"Nonsense! Rubbish! Poppycock!"

interrupted Dr Swill. "Nurse Pinky's so BORING! No wonder I never notice her. She never has any fun. I've seen more life in a limp lettuce!"

Suddenly there was a click and a flash, and someone from the newspaper took their picture. What a picture it made: Nurse Pinky, her face smeared with chocolate; a dishevelled Dr Swill, his white coat torn and stethoscope askew; and Eddie, a little pig wearing a baseball cap.

Alistair and Alfred had made a hasty retreat outside.

The van was still where they had left it, and so too was the pizza. It was looking a little the worse for wear, but it was still pretty much intact.

"Right," said Alistair. "Let's go. We've still got time to get the pizza to Fred's warehouse before it gets dark." And they climbed inside the van.

They heard the rapid patter of heavy trotters, and craned round to see Winifred hurrying away from the building, ready to climb into the van. Escape seemed to her the most sensible solution to the mess she'd landed herself in.

A shrill voice stopped her in her tracks.

"Winifred! Winifred! Come back here at once, young lady."

It was Mrs Swine, striding across the car park, closely followed by Mr Swine. He was carrying the prize-winning cup.

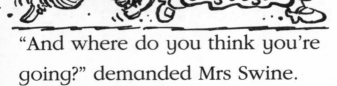

"And where do you think you're going?" demanded Mrs Swine.

"I'm going with Alistair and Alfred," retorted Winifred. "My acting career lies ruined and tattered," she said dramatically, holding a trotter to her forehead.

"Never mind your acting career lying in ruins. What about my beautiful dress? Now *that's* what I call ruined, you naughty, naughty girl."

And with that she marched Winifred off.

Mr Swine had been inspecting the pizza. He gave it a gingerly poke, and then prodded it here and there a little more forcefully.

"Where on earth did this thing come from?" he asked, looking at it closely. Alistair and Alfred glanced at each other, and then Alistair leant

out of the van's window and said in
what he thought was a sincere voice,

"You're not going to believe this,
Dad, but we were driving along,
minding our own business, you
know, like we usually do."

Mr Swine looked
at them doubtfully.

"And this yummy, er, I mean, yukky
mess of a pizza landed right on top
of our van."

"You're right. I don't believe it," said
Mr Swine. "Knowing you two and
your greedy appetites, you probably
came across this pizza by highly
dubious means."

Alistair and Alfred tried to look suitably shocked.

"Now, Dad," said Alfred. "How could you say such a thing? Why, we were just going to take this pizza to where it could be stored. Just until its rightful owner can be found, of course."

"Mmm, well, see that you do," said Mr Swine. "I'd better be getting back inside to make sure everything's calmed down. Goodness me, that sister of yours is even more trouble sometimes than you two put together! Acting, indeed!"

"Take her home, Dad, send her to her room with no tea, we'll eat hers later!" cried the brothers with glee.

Alfred started the engine and began to reverse the rickety old van towards the entrance.

Alfred, as well as being totally useless at most other things, was also a terrible driver. Alistair would never drive as it was bad for his image and creased the arms of his suits too much. So Alfred had to do all the driving.

He should not have been reversing, for the only thing that could be seen out of the back windows was mashed-up squidgy pizza. Alistair finally thought to look out of his side

window, but by then it was much
too late.

"BRAKE! BRAKE!" he shouted.

"Break what?" shouted Alfred back.
"Or do you mean tea break? I could
do with a bite to eat!"

And he put his foot down on the
accelerator instead! Suddenly there
was an almighty crash as Alistair
and Alfred's van hurtled through the
crash barrier and went smack bang

into an oncoming car. The pizza

once again went flying. The guard
ran from his sentry box, still
clutching one of his cheese and
pickle sandwiches, which he had
forgotten to put down in his hurry.

Alistair and Alfred leapt out of their
van to discover what had happened
to their pizza. It had landed upright
this time, and
through it the
outline of a short
figure could be seen,
with arms and legs
outstretched and the
face encased in
dough. The figure stood rigid as the
security guard pulled some of the
pizza away to reveal the extremely
red face of Mr Pedro-Brown.

"Oh dear," said Alistair frowning and peering at Mr Pedro-Brown. "Oh deary, deary me." He shook his head sympathetically, and Mr Pedro-Brown shook his in rage.

"GET THIS PIZZA OFF ME!" he growled.

The security guard made no move to assist him. He stood there, still mesmerised, with his sandwich held midway towards his open mouth.So Alistair and Alfred set to work extracting Mr Pedro-Brown from his pizza. Slowly, very slowly, they began rolling it down from the top, so that when they had finished it lay at Mr Pedro's feet, rolled up like a tatty old carpet. "There," said Alfred, dusting himself down. "No harm done. It's as good as new."

Mr Pedro-Brown reached boiling point.

"My pizza is ruined!" he raged. "It lies at my feet, like some..." he paused, jumping up and down, pointing towards it, lost for words.
"Like some hideous overgrown swiss roll!" He glared at Alistair and Alfred.

"Hmm," said Alistair thoughtfully, "maybe if we unrolled it..."
"LEAVE IT ALONE!" roared Mr Pedro-Brown. "You've done enough damage!"

"My brother was only trying to help," said Alfred indignantly and he looked at the security guard, who was still rooted to the same spot.

"Don't you want that sandwich, mate?" asked Alfred, and before the guard could utter a word, Alfred snatched it out of his hand and stuffed it in his mouth.

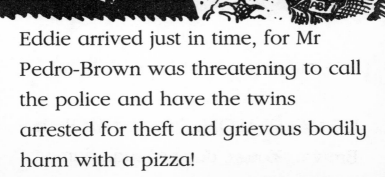

Eddie arrived just in time, for Mr Pedro-Brown was threatening to call the police and have the twins arrested for theft and grievous bodily harm with a pizza!

"You promised the safe return of my pizza," he implored Eddie.

"I know, I know," said Eddie. "And I'm sure my brothers had every intention of returning the pizza to you, Mr Pedro-Brown."

Eddie glanced at the twins, but they said nothing.

"That's as maybe, but they still stole it," said Mr Pedro-Brown. "And that's breaking the law, in my book."

"Ah, yes," replied Eddie carefully. "But they didn't really steal it, did they, Mr Pedro-Brown? A person, or persons whose identity is unknown, performed that dastardly deed."

Mr Pedro-Brown looked thoughtful.
Both he and Eddie looked at Alistair
and Alfred, who had been silent for
some time and were starting to look
a little strange. The pair of them
were changing from a normal
healthy pink colour to a rather
washed-out grey.

Alfred began to groan and hold his
stomach, and Alistair did the same.

"What on earth's wrong with those
two?" asked Mr Pedro-Brown
suspiciously.

Alistair and Alfred groaned again.

"Oh my goodness!" exclaimed Eddie, looking at his brothers. "What was in that pizza? I think they've both been poisoned!"

CHAPTER SIX

Alistair and Alfred had indeed been poisoned – food poisoned – pizza poisoned!

They were both kept in hospital and were put into beds next to each other in the ward.

Mr Pedro-Brown was feeling very guilty, and rather relieved that his pizza had not been eaten by more people so he sent a large basket of fruit. Alistair and Alfred turned their snouts up.

"Fruit," declared Alistair, "is for wombats, monkeys and other tree-climbing idiots. Not for stodge-eating robust, macho pigs!"

So they tried to sell the fruit off individually to the other patients in the ward; an apple here, an orange there, in order to buy sweets and other unhealthy goodies for themselves in the shop downstairs.

Mr and Mrs Swine arrived with Winifred and Eddie at visiting time, and Mrs Swine set about smoothing the bedclothes and ruffling the twins' pillows. She felt their foreheads and generally fussed around them.

"Oh my poor darlings," she kept saying. "My poor, poor darlings."

Winifred was still sulking over her thwarted plans to star in "Heartache Hospital", though she had decided the role of Nurse Pinky was far too wet and weedy for her anyway. Besides, that Dr Swill had had really bad breath. It smelt of antiseptic, ugh!

No, she was now setting her sights on another soap opera, called "The Bean Clan", about the rise and fall, and rise again, of a baked-bean  factory-owning family. Winifred was certain she was just right for the part of Bunty Bean, the beautiful but headstrong daughter!

In her trotter she held that week's local newspaper, and she proudly showed Alistair and Alfred the front page. On it were two huge photographs, one of Nurse Pinky seated in between Dr Swill and Eddie, her face plastered in chocolate. The other showing Winifred in full force, pushing Nurse Pinky ominously towards the chocolate gateau.

The headline read:

NURSE PINKY IN JEALOUS PIG CHOC SHOCK!!!

"Quite a good picture, don't you think?" said Winifred proudly. "Of course, they didn't take my best side."

"And what side would that be then, Winifred?" asked Alfred nastily. "The only good picture you take is one in the dark, with a paper bag over your head!"

Winifred started bashing Alfred

about the ears with the rolled-up
newspaper.

"Stop it! Stop it!" cried Alfred, trying
to defend himself with a plastic
orange-squash bottle. "You'll crease
my pyjamas!"

Mrs Swine split them both up, taking
Winifred briskly off to join Mr Swine
in the hospital canteen.

Eddie sat down on the edge of Alistair's bed.

"I've smoothed things over with Dr Swill," he said, "and Mr Pedro-Brown's just relieved he didn't make the whole town ill, only you two. But you must never do that sort of thing again. Kidnapping is a serious offence, you know," said Eddie sternly.

"Yes, yes," said Alistair with little interest.

He was not grateful to Eddie for sorting things out on behalf of Alfred and himself, and he had other, far more important matters on his mind. As Eddie got up to leave, he grabbed hold of his arm.